Homeland

By

Robert H. (Bob) Keprta

Copyright © 2025 by Robert H. (Bob) Keprta

Books Academy LLC
112 SW HK Dodgen Loop,
Temple, Texas 76504
Hotline: (254) 800-1189

Ordering Information:

Quantity sales. Special discounts are available on quantity purchases by corporations, associations, and others. For details, contact the publisher at the address above.

Printed in the United States of America.

ISBN-13: Softcover 978-1-966567-51-6
Hardcover 978-1-966567-61-5
eBook 978-1-966567-52-3

Library of Congress Control Number: 2024923911

Inspired by True Events

The bow of the ship pierced the early morning fog as Frank leaned against the bulkhead, straining his eyes to get a first glimpse of Hamburg. Hamburg, a city he left years ago as a young lad, only that time he was leaning against the stern of the ship; straining to keep sight of the port city as it slipped farther and farther from view as the ship moved slowly down the Elbe to the sea. That was over two dozen years ago, all the way back in 1901 when he was just 10 years old, accompanied by this papa and mama on the way to America.

On that trip Frank's family traveled in the steerage class, which was in the bowels of the ship. It was hot, poorly ventilated, and very crowded. Sickness and disease were common and spread easily. Whenever they could, they would venture topside to see the ocean and breathe the salty air. Frank envied the first- and second-class passengers, mainly because of the food. Food in steerage was served cafeteria style and usually consisted of boiled potatoes and bread. Sometimes there was sausage and boiled stringy beef. And bread, sometimes very dry bread. There were few tables and those were mostly left to the women and children. Men ate standing up or wherever they could find something to sit on, usually where they slept.

Often passengers would get sick shortly after eating and lose their food on the floor before they could make it to one of the buckets provided for such use. There it would remain unless the person who had produced the mess was well enough to clean it up. Sometimes it remained the entire day as there seemed to be a shortage of porters to keep the area clean. Or maybe there was a shortage of will power for the porter to clean up someone else's vomit. The stench filled the air and was accompanied by the smell of bedding wet from perspiration or urine. It was hard for anyone to endure and made the remaining passengers to become ill themselves. Frank struggled to make it through the day with his food intact, and there were at least 5 more days of the same to look forward to.

Now Frank was returning as a first-class passenger. What a difference, especially the food. Preparation was more meticulous and the fare was more like one would find in a restaurant, properly seasoned and cooked to perfection. In first class dining was at tables and food was served by stewards. The smell of the ocean permeated the dining area and made the experience much more enjoyable, unlike the stench of the steerage class accommodations. The trip back to Hamburg was much more pleasant than the trip leaving Hamburg twenty-some-odd years earlier. It was a much better trip this time by far. Yet Frank could not help but think of the plight of those passengers who could not afford a first-class ticket and were relegated to the steerage class by reason of poverty.

Hamburg was the largest, busiest city that young Frank had ever seen, his eyes could hardly take in all the sights to see and his ears echoed with the clattering sounds of commerce mingled with the ship's horns in the harbor. When he had originally left many years ago, he was in such wonderment of the moment that it was hard to comprehend it all. What an adventure that was! Now he had the time and opportunity to take in every moment of the trip, and what a trip it was!

This return trip was quite different, first he caught a train from Texas, where his family had settled and where he grew up. The train carried him all the way to New Orleans, where he had to change trains to complete the trip to New York. New Orleans was a busy terminal and Frank worried about missing his connection to New York, there was little time to look around as he certainly did not want to miss his connection and must endure an eight-hour wait for the next train in the station that reeked of diesel fumes.

But worrying about missing his connection was not the only thing on his mind; who knew what dangers may lie ahead? Only ten years previous, the "unsinkable" Titanic sank in 1912. On its maiden voyage! Frank had pushed such thoughts of tragedy out of his mind and feasted on the wonderment of the moment. After all, harboring such thoughts would only increase his rising anxiety and spoil the trip. He adopted a "what will be will be" attitude to insulate himself for such concerns. And, above all, he committed himself into God's hands for safekeeping.

Frank's family had decided to leave their homeland and migrate to America because of the abounding tales of opportunity and wealth in the United States. Well, maybe it was more his father Joseph's idea and dream that propelled the family into the unknown, and not that of his mother Mary. She was not the risk taker that Joseph was. But the persistent rumors and talk around the community about vast amounts of land to be had, and the riches waiting in America for those bold enough to seek it out finally won her over to Joseph's nagging. So, selling what little they had they were able to travel to Hamburg and book passage to the United States. Frank recalled his father counting what little money they had left after paying for the ocean liner fare; ten dollars and fifty cents. Ten dollars and fifty cents American on which to enter a bold new chapter in their lives. Mary was concerned about how they could start a new life in a new land with only ten dollars and fifty cents.

Joseph did not share her concerns, however; he had a neighbor friend who had migrated to America years before and it was through his letters that Joseph finally decided to take the risk, for better or worse. Always the optimist, Joseph reassured Mary that all would work out ok, they just had to make it to Ellinger, Texas, where his friend worked at a cotton gin and promised to get Joseph employment there. It was the same friend that vouched for Joseph and agreed to be the family's sponsor for Joseph to secure the passports for the journey.

America, the land across the sea that sent back visions of a better life. A land of opportunities; land to be had for farming. Joseph had made a meager living for his family as a plotnic, a plot farmer. They had enough land to plant some potatoes and cabbages to be used for the table and traded for other goods needed. There was also a small pen of rabbits that furnished fresh meat for the table. And a cow. Everyone had to have a cow for milk and butter, along with a few chickens for eggs. Besides, one cannot have a diet of just rabbit meat; chicken was just as important! Beef was a luxury they could not afford.

But a plotnic was all that Joseph could ever hope to be here in this rural area of the Austria-Hungary Empire. Joseph yearned for more, much more. He wanted a better life for his children when they grew up. He wanted to be able to harvest the fruit of his labor unconstrained by the political and social system into which he was born. That is why the call of the new land was so strong, he wanted to farm more than what he had, to be able to prosper and provide his family all those things he could not here in the homeland. The unknown always fosters fears and concern, and this trip certainly had its share of both. But the hopes and dreams of a better life was enough to overcome the fears and uncertainty that lay ahead.

It has been said that people who are comfortable do not change. Joseph was not comfortable, he was very uncomfortable. He was ready to undertake the rigors, the hardships, the unknowns, of moving to a new land despite the doubts and fears he held within himself….and those that mama did not withhold. They did not know the language. They had little money. They did not know the laws and customs of America. They had never been on a ship before, much less out of sight of land for six days or so. But, after selling what they could not take with them, they set out by cart to Hamburg to begin this new adventure. All that they now possessed was a large blue trunk with clothes and a few treasured keepsakes. And enough money to pay their passage with very little left over. In fact, Frank recalls his papa remarking that they only had ten dollars and fifty cents when they landed in Galveston.

From Galveston, Joseph was able to barter transportation on an ox-cart in exchange for helping with the animals at the end of the day. Mama also assisted in cooking for the group and both chipped in to gather firewood needed for cooking and then combined their efforts for cleaning up everything after the meal. Water was reserved for drinking and all cleaning had to be done in a small stream that flowed nearby. It was important to choose a campsite next to a stream for such purposes.

Once everything was done and put away in its place, they would bed down for the night. Upon arising, the same routine was repeated over again. It took over eight days to travel from Galveston to Columbus, Texas, more time than it took the steam ship to cross the Atlantic. The team master of the caravan that Joseph had arranged to transport him and his family tried to average fifteen miles per day in traveling by ox-cart. At Columbus, the caravan broke up with different families going in different directions, the team master was going to go on toward Austin, but there was still a day's travel from Columbus to Ellinger. The team master told Joseph his help was not needed any further due to the reduction in size of the caravan. He could not take them any further.

But Joseph knew he and his family could not walk the fifteen miles to Ellinger, especially with that large blue trunk which could not be carried or dragged. Reluctantly, Joseph negotiated with the team master to transport them as far as Ellinger, but it cost Joseph five dollars of the meager amount of cash he had left. There was no other choice so Joseph counted out five dollars and paid the man.

At Ellinger, Joseph contacted his old friend at the cotton gin. Sure, enough they were willing to hire Joseph and the family could stay at the friend's house on makeshift pallets until they could get a place of their own. Joseph only worked at the gin for a little over a week when he found better paying employment from one of the cotton farmers who came to the gin to sell their cotton.

Now Frank was returning to the homeland that he had left with his father, mother, and younger sister on a day gleaming with sunshine in what seemed to be so long ago. It was a happy time. The countryside was blooming with wildflowers, small patches of land were bright green with newly sprouting vegetables, and the Sun seemed to shine more brightly. It was a good omen for the coming trip, Frank thought, newness all around; bright and shiny.

Perhaps it was the wanderlust in his blood, inherited from his father. Maybe it was, as he told himself, to visit the cousins he played with as a youngster and see how things had fared with them. Perhaps it was to confirm his father's choice to pull up and leave everything, to confirm that it was a good choice, one he could be proud of. After all, he now had a new suit of clothes, money in his pocket, a paid round-trip passage, an American Passport, and tales to tell of the wondrous life in America.

Now he was returning, a grown man of 31, having spent most of his youth and young adult years in America. His mama and papa had settled in a small town of Ellinger, west of Houston. There they share-cropped on a small cotton farm. It was there that Frank met the love of his life, a young lady named Bosinia, whom he affectionately called "Bo."

Soon after they got married and moved to Sealy, where he had found work as a carpenter's apprentice. When his apprenticeship was over, he became a full-fledged, competent carpenter. Then later moving on to Rosenberg, even closer to the big city of Houston, which, in a way, reminded him of his first experience with Hamburg.

As the ship pierced through the fog getting closer and closer to Hamburg, Frank thought back on his life in Texas. He recalled how his father, Joseph, being a skilled carpenter, found it was easy to find work there. New houses were under construction almost everywhere. And where some could not afford a new home, Joseph found work remodeling and expanding existing homes that had grown too small for an expanding family. It was there in Rosenberg that Joseph stumbled into a new line of work for his carpentry skills.

As opportunity had it, Joseph learned of an abandoned house that was condemned by the city and was to be sold by auction and torn down. It could be had by the highest bidder on the courthouse steps. Joseph was frugal and had saved all his extra income to build his own house for his family. Besides, his son Frank had taken an interest in carpentry and assisted his father at every opportunity. But this abandoned home presented a unique opportunity to acquire lumber at a below market price. He could use the lumber for remodeling and expansion projects, increasing his profit rather than purchasing new lumber at a much higher price.

Joseph and his son Frank were at the courthouse steps early. A small crowd had already begun to gather. As more individuals joined the crowd, Joseph surveyed his potential competition in the bidding for the abandoned home. He paid particular attention to their hands. Were they rough and calloused, indicating hard work, or smooth and soft looking? Joseph was able to further evaluate each person by introducing himself and offering to shake hands, a gesture of friendship not often refused in Texas. Gripping another's hand in a handshake allowed Joseph to further evaluate his competition. To those who he felt would offer the fiercest competition, Joseph cleverly began to sow seeds of doubt into their minds with comments about problems and obstacles he saw in dismantling the building. He mentioned such things as wondering how old and brittle the aged wood would be, which might cause much splintering and loss of wood.

It was not long before the county sheriff appeared at the top of the steps above the crowd and announced the property up for bid. He asked for an opening bid of several thousand dollars. There were no takers. The Sheriff dropped the bid lower, then lower again.   Finally, out of desperation, he asked for a simple one-hundred-dollar bid. Now there was a taker and the bidding quickly rose to three hundred dollars. Then the bidding inched higher and higher, first at fifty dollar increments and then twenty-five until it reached five hundred dollars. The man that Joseph had suspected of being the toughest competition was the high bidder.   Joseph held back until after the "going three times" announcement was made and just before the gavel came down to end the sale, Joseph announced,

"seven hundred dollars." The jump in increments from the previous twenty-five-dollar amounts worked and no one challenged Joseph's seriousness about buying the property. No further bids.

"Sold for seven hundred dollars" the Sheriff announced as the gavel came down. Frank had learned something that day, watching how his father worked the crowd and conducted his bidding. Knowledge that would prove invaluable in years to come. Frank learned something else as well, prior to attempting to dismantle the building, Joseph had Frank climb upon the roof of the building with a small rope dangling behind him. Then Joseph tied the lower end of the rope to a lawn sprinkler attached to a long garden hose and had Frank pull it up to the top of the structure. After Frank climbed down, Joseph turned on the water supply and began soaking the house with water. Joseph explained to Frank that the water would cause the boards to swell, making the nails pull out easier and saving much wood from splintering. The plan was to "sprinkle" the house for approximately two days to allow the water to seep inside the house as well.

A sudden sharp blast from the ship's fog horn jarred Frank from his reminiscing. The early morning fog began to melt away under the brightness of the rising sun as the ship pushed further up the Elbe toward Hamburg. On the way to America, the ship sailed out of

Hamburg in the daytime so that the trip up the Elbe could be easily navigated by sight, there was no need for the constant fog horn signal of an approaching vessel that could not be seen due to the fog. As a youngster, Frank was fascinated by how the large ship could sail across the ocean and arrive at its designated port.

Navigating across such a huge ocean seemed to be an insurmountable task, but a task the captain of the ship did easily. The ship plowed through the evening fog on the Elbe guided by radio frequency signals. Frank would occasionally look up at the spinning loop on top of the ship's bridge as its radio pierced the fog with its signals, Frank looked up at it occasionally just to reassure himself that it was still spinning, warding off any potential collision! Frank marveled at how much the world had changed from his previous voyage. Collisions were rare, but disastrous when they did occur and he wanted to re-assure himself that all was going well. Frank knew that the ship had to be in the river Elbe, even though he could not see the shoreline or mouth of the river as they approached the port city. The claxon calls of ship's horns and the chugging of powerful engines as other vessels passed slowly by told him that they were in the narrowness of the river and not the vast expanse of ocean they had sailed the last five days.

Occasionally he could catch a glimpse of lights on the left and right. Some were shore lights; some were beacons that also housed the radio transmitters to guide the ship. But how much further to Hamburg Frank had no idea. Yet he maintained his vigil, looking for that first sight of the harbor.

Then, as if some huge curtains were pulled back, the ships at dock and the buildings of the city became visible. Smoke stacks with large plumes of black smoke poured forth into the sky. Some of the smoke stacks were high and tall, made of untold thousands of bricks reaching up and disappearing into the lifting fog. Frank had wondered at them when he first saw them, how was it possible to get those bricks built layer upon layer so high above the ground. There were many ships docked around the port, with smaller boats ferrying between them.

The hustle and clamor of a living world pressed upon him as the sea was left behind and the ship neared the dock. Frank was excited! He had made the journey back toward his homeland and, with the coming of the next day or so, would be seeing old childhood friends again and living and reliving all that had happened since he left so many years ago. Frank went back to his cabin to prepare to embark from his voyage. He paused as he packed his lone suitcase with a few changes of clothes, necessities, and a small New Testament, reminiscing about the big blue trunk into which they had packed all that the family owned.

For a moment he remembered that they had disembarked at Galveston on the Texas coast and that Frank's father commented on the fact that all they had was ten dollars and fifty cents, plus the clothes they wore and those in the trunk. How the world has changed, he thought. Then he grasped the case by its worn leather handle and strode quickly down the aisle to the stairs, up the stairs to the deck, and down the passenger walkway to the dock.

Once ashore, Frank gave a backward glance at the huge ocean liner that made the voyage, it seemed to be twice as large as the one he and his family had departed on years before. And it was much more comfortable.   Before they could only afford steerage class, which was crowded and seemed to be deep down within the bowels of the ship. It made him think about Jonah and his experience in the belly of a great whale or fish of some sort. But this trip back was more in style, he was a first-class passenger and had more freedom to move about the ship. Better sleeping quarters. And better food too!

Checking in with the Ticketmaster at the nearby train depot, Frank bought a ticket to Prague that departed in about an hour. Frank purchased a ticket on the last of three daily trips the trains made to Prague. It was also in his favor that the last train was later in the evening, as the trip would take about 12 hours by rail, this would allow him to sleep on the train instead of spending funds for a night's lodging in Hamburg. It also gave him time to take in the sights of the city for the next hour before boarding the train.

Frank was hungry since the ship did not serve departing passengers a final meal. Frank strolled around the port area, but not venturing too far from the train depot. He was taking in all the sights and smells, but he walked far enough away from the depot to lose the smell of the diesel exhaust from the trains! The smell of food cooking made Frank even more hungry as he passed cafes on the street. One grabbed Frank's attention and he stepped inside to be greeted by a hostess and seated next to a window so he could view the hustle and bustle of the morning commerce up and down the street. He ordered a breakfast, which was served all day, of Kartoffelpuffer (German potato pancakes) which came with a small Brat (sausage) and Kaffee (coffee).

Frank had originally planned to make it from Hamburg to Prague upon arrival, but he had made no provisions to stay in Prague. Still, he would be able to arrive by train in the early morning hours and find lodging before continuing to Kunvald the next day. Kunvald, the town in which he was born. He remembered much of it as it was such a small village at the time. Small shops and markets surrounded by many small farms and old houses. He remembered that the house in which he grew up was much like a barn with living quarters above. The animals got the first floor with all the living quarters above.

Frank had traveled alone. Bo was insistent that she would not make the trip. It reminded him of squabbles Joseph would have with his mother before they finally came to terms and sailed for America. But Bo was born in America and the homeland of Czechoslovakia did not have the draw on her as it did Frank. Frank shook his head as if to clear the thoughts from his head, soon he would be back on the way home to them. He planned on staying only a day or so in Kunvald. He felt confident he could find overnight lodging in Kunvald with one of his old friends. Most of his time away from Bo would be spent in travel.

After eating, Frank ambled back to the train station and boarded his scheduled train. Frank looked for a seat with no nearby passengers so he could sleep instead of engaging in conversation. Soon the conductor came by and asked for Frank's ticket.

"Are you from Prague?" the conductor asked.

"No, Kunvald" Frank replied.

Conductor: "How long ago did you leave Czechoslovakia?"

"Just over twenty years," Frank replied.

"You will find much has changed, and not all for the better," said the Conductor.

With that Frank settled back on his seat and using his jacket as a pillow, tried to go to sleep, wondering what the Conductor had meant by "not all for the better." He thought that maybe there had been a great fire, maybe some turbulent storm destroyed the town. Would he find his boyhood home still standing? The rhythmic clacking of the rails kept him awake, but the last words of the conductor kept bouncing around in his head, almost in meter with the clacking of the rails. "Not all for the better," Frank pondered, just what did he mean by that? He did not want to ask any questions that would further the conversation. While still wondering about that last comment, he drifted into a sound sleep.

"Prague" came a loud shout as the conductor prodded Frank awake. He was almost home, Kunvald was just a few more hours away. He was not quite sure how he would get there. Surely there was some kind of commercial traffic going through Kunvald to Poland, at least a bus or cab would be available. Bus would be cheaper, he thought. But first, breakfast. The long trip from Hamburg to Prague awakened his appetite. He had not eaten since the breakfast he had in Hamburg the previous evening.

Spotting a small café a few blocks from the train station, Frank found a table, set his suitcase down and waited to be served. A waitress soon came by and placed a menu in front of Frank without speaking a word. There were not many patrons at the café, and soon the waitress approached him again and asked what he desired, speaking in Czech. Frank looked over the menu, and answering in the Czech language, ordered two eggs, scrambled, with a local sausage link. And coffee. Must have coffee.

The eggs and sausage arrived and the waitress, looking at his suitcase, asked, "where are you traveling from?"

"Texas" Frank replied.

"Where is that?" the waitress inquired.

"A state in America, much like a province," Frank reported.

Her eyes widened upon hearing that Frank was from America, and since he had spoken to her in perfect Czech, she knew he or his family were from Czechoslovakia.

"Are you a citizen of America or Czechoslovakia?" she asked.

Frank, "I left here at ten years of age with my parents, I have an application in to become a citizen of the United States but it is still pending, so to answer your question, it would seem that I am still a citizen of Austria-Hungarian Empire since the Czech Republic did not exist at that time but only came about years after I left."

Then Frank wondered about her question concerning citizenship. That seemed overly inquisitive and out of the ordinary as a question to be asked at such a brief encounter. He also pondered why he had divulged so much information about his citizenship to a stranger.

His answer to the waitress seemed to satisfy her as there were no more questions. She resumed her duties around the café. While enjoying his breakfast, Frank noticed the waitress on the telephone as she glanced in Frank's direction but then quickly turned her head away as she caught Frank's eye. He gave it no further thought and was about to finish his meal and leave when two men entered the café wearing long overcoats and brimmed hats. The two men approached the waitress and were engaging in conversation as they also glanced Frank's way. Strange Frank thought, as an uneasiness began to settle over him. Frank rose from his seat to leave, stopping briefly at the main counter to pay for his meal.

As Frank walked to the entrance door, the two men moved to the doorway blocking Frank's exit. "Excuse, please" Frank said in Czech.

"You must answer some questions for us," one of the men said in German.

"And who are you?" Frank asked in German. Frank spoke both Czech and German, but his Czech was more proficient and natural.

"We will ask the questions" came the reply. "Show us your papers," He requested.

Frank, "What papers do you mean?"

"Your papers, your Identification, passport, travel papers, all the papers you have." The second man stated in an agitated tone.

Frank set his suitcase down and reached inside his jacket pocket for his passport. As he did so, the men stiffened in front of him and placed their hands inside their long top coats, exposing pistols that they gripped without removing them from their holsters.

Now Frank was worried. This seemed serious and he did not quite understand what was going on. He handed the passport to one of the men and asked, "What is this all about? I have a legal passport from the United States to visit Czechoslovakia."

One of the men picked up Frank's suitcase and turned to the door while the other one said, "You must come with us." Now Frank was really scared and asked again, "What is this about, I have a legal passport, where are we going?"

"You must explain to the magistrate, we are only following procedure, you will learn what charges are against you when you see the magistrate."

With that they ushered Frank out the door. Four blocks down from the café was the police station and magistrates' office. Frank was ushered down the street with one of the men carrying his suitcase and the other one firmly grasping Frank's arm as if Frank was going to try to escape.

"I do not understand, what is going on, why are you treating me like this, I am a legal tourist, you cannot do this," Frank protested.

To which one of the men said, "Be quiet, you can ask your questions to the magistrate, not to us, you will be told everything in a minute sit here," one of the men said-as they led Frank to a straight-back wood bench inside the office, which also appeared to be a small courtroom.

There was no one else in the office. One of the men put Frank's suitcase on a table and opened it. He rummaged through the contents while the other one picked up a phone and made a call. He talked in a low voice and Frank could not hear the conversation. The one rummaging through the suitcase stuffed Frank's belongings back into it, closed the case, apparently satisfied that what he was looking for was not among the contents.

Frank asked, "Let me see your badges, if you are police or government agents you must have badges."

The man who was talking on the phone insisted that Frank stop asking questions and to be quiet. "The magistrate will be here in a few minutes," he said and left the building, leaving the other to guard the entrance doorway.

Frank sat on the bench wondering what was going on, a thousand questions raced through his mind as he tried to make sense of the situation. Minutes past, but they seemed like hours. Frank lost track of the time.

He began to pray. "Heavenly Father, I do not know what is happening here, please help me, I need your help now." He prayed for understanding, that this was all some sort of mix up in identification or something. Whatever was causing this situation, he prayed for it to be resolved so he could be on his way to Kunvald to see his relatives and friends. And after that, return to Texas and his family. His family, his beloved wife Bo, and their two-year-old daughter Emilie. What if he never was able to return home, he thought, Emilie will grow up never knowing her father, and how much I love her and her mother. Frank's disposition darkened as such thoughts invaded his consciousness.

At last, the magistrate appeared through an inner door and took his place behind the elevated bench just short of the back wall. He spoke to the man guarding the entrance door, and the guard proceeded to where Frank was sitting and commanded him to stand up, and with a firm grasp on Frank's arm, jerked him in front of the Judge's bench. The magistrate fumbled through some papers, apparently reading a little here and there.

Finally, the Judge looked Frank in the eye and said, "You are charged with deserting your homeland in time of crises to evade your civic and patriotic duties as a citizen of the Czech Republic. How do you plead, guilty or not guilty?"

Frank was stunned; he had no idea what the Judge was talking about.

"What do you mean," Frank stammered, "I am an American, coming to visit my relatives in Kunvald."

"Are you a citizen of the United States?" The Judge inquired in a quizzical manner, "If so, I must see your legal papers as a citizen of the United States. Where are your papers? Show me your papers or be silent," he demanded.

"Well, your honor, I left this country when I was only ten years old with my father and mother to go to the United States. I have lived there all my life, for the past twenty-one years, I have a wife and child there…"

"Silence," the judge said in a raised, agitated voice. "You are not to speak unless you provide proof that you are not a citizen of this country. You were a citizen of the Austria-Hungarian Empire when you left and are a citizen of that part of the Empire which is now Czechoslovakia until you prove otherwise," the judge said in a belligerent, firm tone.

Frank had a foreboding sense of how serious this situation was becoming and began to pray silently under his breath. "Lord, help me. I need you now Lord, I pray for your guidance and to make this situation go away, please make things right Lord so I can return to my wife and little girl."

"Are you, or are you not, still a citizen of this country," the judge demanded while glaring down at Frank with a stern, fixed gaze. "You are a citizen somewhere, where is that somewhere?" the judge continued.

"Well, your honor…. technically speaking I still am but I…." Frank stammered to make sense of the situation

The judge suddenly interrupted Frank with, "so by your own admission, you are a citizen of Czechoslovakia. For desertion of your country in time of need during the great war"

"But I was only 10 years old, in the accompaniment of my parents, what else was I to do?" Frank questioned.

Ignoring Frank's question the judge proceeded, "For dissertation of your country in time of need and due to the current looming crises between Germany and the Czech Republic, you are sentenced to 6 years of military service, and be glad it is not 6 years in prison. That is all. Guards, escort him to the military barracks 2 miles east of Prague and turn him over to the provost there." Spoke to the judge as he rose to exit the room as if all were settled in this matter.

No sooner had the judge spoken the words than the two guards, which were now standing beside him, firmly grasped his arms and spun Frank around towards the door.

As they walked Frank toward the door, Frank exclaimed, "but my suitcase and all of my clothes and things, and I want my passport back!"

The judge shouted back at Frank, "You have no need of them now, you will get new clothes at the barracks, and your passport is invalid, if you wish to leave this country in the future you must obtain a passport from the Czech Republic, and we are not issuing any new passports at this time, besides, it will be 6 years before you can inquire."

Looking over his shoulder on the way to the door, Frank saw someone enter the room and take his suitcase, it was the lady at the restaurant who waited on Frank. The one who asked about his citizenship. The one he had seen talking to the two secret police. Now Frank began to make sense of her questions regarding his citizenship, she must be working with the government agents, and as a reward, she received all the person's belongings if they were incarcerated.

Frank's heart sank within him. How could things be going so bad? He wondered why he had such a drive within him to visit his homeland when all this trouble was in store. Why has this happened? Why? Why? Frank was at a loss to make sense of the situation. Once outside, he was guided to step onto the open back of a transport truck, it had no canvas cover over the cargo area and no tailgate. He had difficulty believing that all this was happening, it was like a bad dream, but no, he was not dreaming. He pinched himself to make just to make sure. No, it was not a bad dream, it was reality. A reality that caused him to wonder if he would ever see his wife and daughter again. How he missed them! How wonderful and fortunate it was that Bosinia did not come with him and be subjected to this ordeal.

A sudden bounce as the truck hit a hole in the road jarred him back to the present. I must have a plan, he thought. Think! Think! There must be a way to get back to America and his family, a way to escape from this madness. He looked around at the passing countryside to get his bearings. The judge said the barracks was on the east side, look North and find some landmarks to remember, he thought. All he could see were non-descript houses and barns, then they crossed a little stream. Suddenly Frank remembered his father telling him that all water flowed to the sea. The stream must be flowing North since Hamburg and the Elbe were to the North. Maybe the stream flowed into the Elbe, or if not, to some tributary that did flow into the Elbe.

Only a short distance more and the barracks was in sight. It was a cold, dreary looking place. At the entrance roadway there were two sentries posted. One on either side of a lift arm type of barricade across the road. The truck stopped. The driver told the sentries why they were there. One of them walked to the back of the truck and looked up at Frank. Then looking around at the guards who were with Frank, he nodded his head and the barricade was lifted for the truck to proceed on to the barracks grounds. As they went through the checkpoint, Frank thought it odd that there was a guarded road into the barracks site, with a barricade but no fence around the compound. In the distance he could see the tree line of the stream they had crossed. Frank calculated in his mind that it was about a half mile across open ground to the stream. He stored that information in his memory as the truck stopped again in front of the barracks headquarters building.

Outside was a guard with two sentry dogs. German Shepherds. That is why there is no fence, Frank thought. They have guard dogs as a fence! Inside the building, Frank was presented to the front desk clerk along with some papers from the court. The stern-looking, balding person in charge looked at the papers, then at Frank, then back down to the papers. He said something in Czech to an obvious orderly seated nearby and the orderly got up and left. He soon returned with a uniformed person who was armed with a pistol on his belt.

The guards who had transported Frank were dismissed. As they were leaving the building, the new guard was given instructions in Czech. Frank understood perfectly what was said, he was to be placed in building B-1 until further transport to a Military base. This was apparently a temporary holding barracks for incoming personnel. Frank asked the person in charge how long he would be here. "A week, maybe two" the man answered. "Until there are enough recruits to form a new unit, then you will be transported to the military base and begin training as a unit."

As Frank thought of his situation, he realized in his mind that if he were to somehow escape, it would be easier here than at a better guarded military installation, which would probably have a fence. But how? I have to stay calm and develop a plan, Frank thought.

Once checked in, Frank was escorted to a supply building where he was ordered to strip, "Take off your shirt and pants," he was told. Once he had done so, they were handed to a clerk behind a long running counter. The clerk stretched out his shirt by the two cuffs, placed the collar up to his neck and seemed to be determining the size based on how Frank's shirt measured up to his own physique. He did the same with the pants and then threw both onto a pile of clothes behind the counter. He walked away, disappearing between and behind shelves of military style clothing. He soon returned with a shirt and pants and tossing them across the counter to Frank, said, "Try these on." Catching the tossed clothes in the air, Frank asked, "Does everyone here speak only Czech?"

"Where do you think you are, Italy?" came a sarcastic reply to which the guards and everyone in the building laughed. Frank tried the new clothes on, they seemed to be a reasonably good fit based on the cursory measurements made by the clerk. He must have had lots of experience in this, Frank thought. The makeshift uniform was not new, the sleeves and shoulders evidenced where previous emblems of unit and rank had once been sewn.

Then he was escorted to building B-1 where he was assigned an empty bunk. Looking around it seemed to Frank that the other occupants of B-1 were much younger than him. Speaking to the person sitting on the bunk next to him, Frank asked how long he had been there.

"Just today." Came the response.

Frank wondered about the circumstances that caused this young man to be there. They engaged in small talk about where each was from and their families, what they liked to do, and so on. Frank learned that his name was Karl, and that he was born in Prague. When it came to talking about the government or military, Karl abruptly stopped all conversation and remained quiet.

"Did you volunteer for the military or were you conscripted," Frank questioned.

"You might say I am a volunteer," the young man replied. "I was convicted of a crime and the judge gave me a choice between two years in prison or three years in the military. I chose the military, so in that sense you could say I am a volunteer."

Then Karl continued, "Do not question about the government or military," Karl cautioned in a barely audible whisper. "It will only cause trouble for you," he continued.

"So, what do we do during the day," Frank asked of Karl.

"It is a work camp for new recruits and inductees" came the reply. We are all assigned to different work crews to maintain the compound. You will soon be placed in a work crew until transport arrives to take us to the military base, depending on when they are ready to form another unit," Karl replied.

Soon a whistle blew. "Time to eat," Karl said, "follow me outside for formation and do as I do."

Outside the commander of unit B-1 instructed the new arrivals to form lines with the others, with ten persons to a line. Frank wound up in a line different from the one Karl was in. Once the shuffling about to create the formation settled down, the unit commander counted the total number of people in the formation. Ten to a line made it easier for him to arrive at a total head count. Looking down at the clipboard he carried, he satisfied himself that all was in order. Then he marched the group to the cafeteria for lunch.

Inside Frank followed suit with what the person in front of him did. Picking up a tray, he walked through the food line. He received a portion of boiled potatoes, some dark colored beans, and a slice of bread. It looked like the food that Frank had in the steerage section of the ship he had immigrated to America on. He sat down at a table with the man who was in front of him in the line. Tasting the food, which had no taste, Frank commented that the food was not very good.

"That is why there is plenty of salt and pepper on the tables." He was told.

Frank asked for the salt and pepper to be passed to him as they were on the far end of the table. Without anything being spoken, the person on the end of the table looked in Frank's direction and slid the shakers down the table to him. Frank put salt and pepper on his food. As he was shaking the pepper out of the container, Frank suddenly thought he could use pepper to throw the dogs off his trail if he was able to escape. Frank pretended to not be able to get the pepper to shake out of the container. Taking the cap off, he banged it down on his napkin pretending to open the clogged pores. Then he "accidentally" spilled some pepper onto his napkin as he replaced the cap. No one appeared to notice so Frank folded the napkin in half and then in half again, covering the pepper. Frank had nearly finished his meal when the person in charge of B-1 shouted "Two minutes" then two minutes later shouted for everyone to clear the tables and move outside.

As Frank stood up, he reached down for his tray and grasped the folded napkin in one hand with the tray in the other. On the way to turn in his tray to the kitchen, Frank managed to fold the napkin once again and shoved it down into his pocket. Having turned in his tray, Frank again followed what everyone else was doing,

Outside they were forming lines of ten each. The building commander took a head count and having assured himself that all were present, dismissed them to join their work crews.

There were several small groups of persons from other barracks whose overseer was standing in front of each group. Now Frank did not know what to do, so he asked, "What crew do I go to?"

"What do you do, what kind of work have you done before?" "I am a carpenter" Frank replied.

"Not a farmer, huh. Good! You are assigned to the crew on the far left." The man replied.

Joining that crew, Frank went with them to a barracks that had fallen, whether by storm or age Frank could not tell. Once there, he was given a hammer and told to pull nails out of boards that were removed from the shambles and sort them by size and dimension. The rest of the crew engaged themselves in removing boards from the disheveled pile that once was a building and casting them aside away from their work area.

Frank began picking up the boards and removing the nails. Suddenly it dawned on him that he did not know what to do with the nails. Inquiring of the crew manager, he was told that they go in the bucket next to a burn pile where scraps of lumber and unusable pieces were obviously burned. Frank went about removing nails and sorting boards for the entire afternoon.

During the course of the day's activities, Frank noticed that the building next to the one that had collapsed was abandoned and very dilapidated. Frank asked the crew chief if that building was also to be torn down. "That is not of your concern, your duty is to clean the lumber in this stack and sort it by dimensions, so get back to work" the crew chief commanded in a harsh tone.

Frank voluntarily said, "Well, if it was to be torn down, I would offer to make a suggestion. If you could locate a water sprinkler and out it atop the building with the water on, the dry wood would swell making it easier to take apart as the dry wood clinches onto the nails. It would also reduce splintering and loss of wood in the process."

"Listen you," the crew chief growled, "if I want your opinion on how to run this detail, I will ask for it, and I didn't ask so no more grumbling and get back to work." The next morning Frank had to smile and chuckle to himself as they marched to the clean-up site, for he noticed a water sprinkler on top of the next building wetting it down! But Frank knew better than to say anything about his making that suggestion. Let the crew chief take the credit. It reminded him of a saying his father used to use, "it's amazing how much can be accomplished if no one worries about who gets the credit." To Frank, it did not matter who got the credit, the end result was it made Frank's and the rest of the crew's work easier.

At the end of the work day, it was always the same. Put up all the tools. Evening meal. Then to the barracks, clean everything, sweep, mop, and go to bed. The same routine, day after day. It became monotonous.

His first night was virtually sleepless as Frank pondered his situation, prayed, thought of his family, and then prayed some more. He was only planning a short trip to the homeland, but now his family would soon know something was wrong when he did not return on the date scheduled. Maybe they will think he is dead, he thought. He prayed for their protection in his absence and for the Lord to guide him home again. Finally, he went into a restless sleep and almost as suddenly was rudely awakened by yelling and shouting. It was a uniformed person who apparently replaced the former building commandant, who was now in charge of building B-1. All were to make their beds and be ready to line up for breakfast in 10 minutes.

Day after day it was the same routine, get up, breakfast, pull nails, stack boards, lunch break, evening meal, go to bed. The routine never changed, always the same thing, over and over and over. Frank wondered when he and the others would be shipped to the military base to form a new unit. During each meal time Frank managed to smuggle a small amount of pepper out of the cafeteria. He kept it stored inside of his pillow case, daily adding to the amount of pepper he had accumulated. One morning during this mundane routine, Frank was eating the meager breakfast provided when someone he had not previously talked to came over and sat next to him.

While eating, the man said to Frank, "Are you a Christian?" without looking up from his tray of food.

"Yes" answered Frank, "What made you ask?"

"I saw you praying before every meal," he continued. "Do you read the Bible?" he asked further.

"Whenever I can" Frank responded.

"Tomorrow at this same time, sit in this same place and I will give you a few pages of Scripture, when you finish reading them, pass them back to me and I will give you a few more, the pages will be kept in circulation among the Christians here as long as possible," the man said.

The next morning Frank did as the man said. When the man, whose name he learned was Gerhard, sat beside him and slid some folded pages to Frank from under his tray. Frank pushed them under his own tray. Without saying anything, the man finished eating and rose to return his tray to the kitchen. As Frank rose, he discreetly put the folded pages, which were small enough to be covered in the palm of his hand, into his pocket.

Later in the day Frank got permission to leave the detail and go to the toilet facilities. Once there, Frank locked himself into a stall as if he were going to use the facilities and pulled the folded pages out of his pocket. It was two pages from the book of Philippians. Verses 4:13 was underlined, "I can do all things through Christ who strengthens me. Verse 4:19 was also underlined, "And my God shall supply all your need through His riches in glory by Christ Jesus."

But what immediately caught Frank's eye and attention was a note written in the margin, "God will provide." Frank's heart leaped within himself for it was Frank's own handwriting and he remembered immediately having written that note to himself in his own New

Testament which was in the suitcase confiscated when he was brought before the magistrate! How wonderful are the ways of God! How past searching out are His workings!

Almost as immediately, as he had thought these thoughts, he recalled the instance in the Old Testament where Joseph confronted his brothers in Egypt. Once he had identified himself as their brother whom they had jealously thrown in a pit and the sold into slavery; he told them that they had meant it for evil but God had meant it for good! God's ways are so far above our ways that they are impossible for us to understand. Frank felt renewed energy and hope welling up within himself. He now had confidence that he would make it back to America and to his beloved Bo and daughter Emilie.

Returning to the detail he pulled nails and stacked lumber with a new vigor, almost breaking out in happiness. He noticed others glancing at him as they completed their tasks as if something strange had happened to him. And it had! Frank's attitude and work exuded happiness in all his doings. Later Frank confided in Karl what had happened and Karl was equally astounded. Surely God in all His mercy had not abandoned them.

Later that evening as Frank lay on his bunk bed, he thought again of the marvelous things that had happened that day. He again returned to thinking out his plan to escape and get back to his family. Frank recalled the stream which was on the West side of the camp. If he could find a way to leave the barracks at night and cross the open field to the stream, he would walk along the stream's East side searching for a tree. It had to be a specific tree, one with branches stretching out over the bank and branches stretching out over the stream. The limbs on the bank side had to be low enough for Frank to jump up and grab them and then pull himself up into the tree. He could then crawl along the limb to the trunk, circle around the trunk and out on the limb over the stream and then drop into the stream.

To fool the dogs, Frank thought he would pass the tree up for a way, scatter the pepper in a relatively open area away from the bank. Then he could carefully backtrack his steps to the tree, jump up and grab the limb and make it into the stream which would cover his scent. That might fool the trackers once the dogs reacted to the pepper. With his trail ending abruptly, it may fool the dogs and trackers for a while anyway before they could figure out what Frank had done. It would gain him time.

But the first order of business was to get out of the barracks. Frank got up and went to the latrine as if he had to use the facilities. It was early in the morning hours, and as Frank walked slowly down the middle of the barracks, it appeared that everyone was fast asleep. He checked the doors at the end of the barracks and found that they were unlocked. The barracks had doors on both ends. On one end was the latrine and on the other was a private room where the barracks commander slept. It was good that the doors on the latrine side were unlocked, there would be less chance of waking the commander as Frank opened the creaky doors to escape.

Were the doors always unlocked? Frank thought so but he did not know. Perhaps the commander had forgotten to lock these doors, or maybe it was God who unlocked the doors just as He had opened the prison cells for Paul and Barnabas. Now was the time to go, Frank thought. Almost immediately he feared being caught and what the consequences would be. Frank hesitated for a moment and then decided that now was the time. He must take the chance.

Returning to his bunk bed, Frank gathered his clothes, his shoes, and his "cache" of pepper which he kept wrapped in a napkin inside of his pillow case. As quietly as he could, he walked down the barracks to the opposite end. Each step made his heart beat faster. What if someone awoke and saw him and called out to him, thereby waking others and soon the entire barracks would be awake with Frank standing in the middle clutching all his clothes! How could he ever explain that!

As fate would have it, someone did awake. Frank stopped dead in his tracks. The person half lifted himself up from his bunk bed and stared at Frank. All the while Frank was praying under his breath. It was Gerhard. After what seemed to be an eternity, Gerhard looked down at the opposite end of the barracks towards the commander's room, looked back at Frank, then reclined back on his bunk and rolled over facing away from Frank. Frank continued down the center aisle of the barracks and slowly opened the door just enough to get outside without causing the door to make its distinctive creak.

Outside Frank put on his clothes, socks, and shoes. Now he crept along the shadow of the barracks on the leeward side to the West end where the commander's room was. All was quiet. At the end of the barracks, he gazed down the open area between the rows of barracks for any signs of life. Having seen none, Frank quickly crossed the open area to the next row of barracks, which was "A" row. The open area between was where morning and evening formations were held. As Frank quickly crossed over to "A" row, he thought about what the morning formation would be like when it would be discovered that he was absent!

He then stayed within the shadow of A-1 until he reached the open field between the camp and the stream. He quickly crossed over to the stream and paused to look behind him for any unusual activity. All was quiet, all was calm; it was like the Christmas carol, nothing was stirring, nothing was moving, not even a mouse! Except Frank. He was moving North along the stream looking for a tree to suit his needs. He passed farmhouses on his right side which were all dark and quiet. After about a mile, Frank found the perfect tree with strong limbs on either side and on the bank side low enough for him to leap up and climb. Just to make sure, Frank made a few "practice" jumps to grasp the limb. He was able to do it and on a trial basis was able to pull himself up high enough to throw a leg over the limb and make it fully up onto the limb.

Dropping himself to the ground, he continued North for about a quarter of a mile, at which time he spread the pepper across the front of his pathway, turned, and then began walking back to the tree. Frank was careful to avoid high grass, as when he backtracked the blades of taller grass would be bent back in the direction of travel, making it evident that he had backtracked. Frank backtracked by walking backwards, carefully placing the toe of his receding foot down first, then rocking back on to the heel. Step after careful step so the grass would always appear bent forward to disguise his ruse. Reaching the tree, Frank leapt up, grasped the limb, and pulled himself up on it. He then carefully crawled along the limb to the trunk. Frank had to climb slightly higher to get to a limb big enough to support him that also reached out over the stream.

Dangling from the limb, Frank looked down at the water surface, he wanted to be careful not to drop onto a floating brush pile or log. The water was moving but not too swiftly, besides, Frank was a strong swimmer. He had spent much time on the river before his family moved to Texas and even more time in the water in Texas. Seeing that the water looked clear, he took a deep breath and let go of the limb. He splashed into the water feet first like a torpedo and quickly was submerged over his head. His feet did not touch bottom as the momentum of the drop slackened and Frank swam up to the top to get another breath. Since he did not hit bottom, he knew that the water may be moving swifter than it seemed. Shallow water made more of a surface disturbance. This was good. Swift water would move him further along quicker.

Fortunately, there were no Water Moccasins in Europe like in Texas. In Texas, these poisonous snakes were also known by the name "Cotton Mouth" as their open mouth was snowy white like cotton when they stretched their jaws wide in preparation for a strike. Frank had encountered them before, but he was never bitten. A friend of his was bitten by one as they played in the water of a small stream in Texas, though his friend did not die, Frank was aware of the long painful recovery his friend had, and he even lost his foot which had to be amputated. Frank did not want to be introduced to any such reptile in the stream into which he had just plunged himself.

Nor was there any threat from alligators such as they had in Texas. In fact, there were many dangers to be avoided in the United States. There were several varieties of poisonous snakes including rattlesnakes, cottonmouths, coral snakes, and copperheads. Alligators were an altogether different peril. As Frank swam down the stream, he encountered a half-sunken log to which he attached himself to float along and save his energy.

Occasionally Frank would move close to the West bank to get a glimpse of the terrain. On one such venture he noticed vehicle lights moving in parallel to the stream only a short distance away. Now a new twist on Frank's plans emerged in his mind. Crawling up the bank he crossed the field towards the roadway. As vehicles came by in either direction, he would stop and lie flat on the ground. Closer to the road he found a ditch which would shield him from the headlights.

When the road was clear of traffic in both directions, he walked up the ditch bank to the pavement. Once on the pavement he crossed to the other side and walked about 10 yards along the shoulder, then slightly out onto the pavement. Then he carefully backtracked to the exact spot he had left the stream, which was becoming more of a small river. Frank thought that if the military suspected that he had entered the stream, they would use dogs on both sides of the water to see where he got out. This twist in Frank's plans would make it seem as if he exited on the West bank, traveled to the road, and there hailed a ride on some vehicle that stopped 10 yards or so from where he stood, then the trail would disappear. It would make it seem as though he had found a ride on a vehicle traveling in the opposite direction than Frank's true plans. His plan was to head North to Hamburg, not South to Prague. Perhaps the trackers would think Frank was delirious or disorientated and did not know which way or where to go. He knew he could not catch a ride North to Hamburg because of the clothes he was wearing. If the people of Hamburg could sense that he was not from there due to his clothes, they would certainly be aware that he had left a military compound and be subject to a possible reward if he was to be found.

Back in the stream, Frank looked for the log but it was gone. The current had carried it further downstream. Frank recalled a survival trick he had learned from a friend in Texas. While in the water, Frank removed his pants and tied a knot in the ends of the trouser legs. Then zipping and buttoning the waist, he held the pants by the top of the waist and slung them over his head. Then with an upward and forward motion, swept them over his head to his front, trapping air in each leg. Putting one of the pants legs that were ballooned with air under each arm, he smoothed the waist under his abdomen. A perfect improvised pair of "Water Wings." The wet cloth would hold air for quite some time, then he would repeat the procedure to refill the legs with air. Now he could move along the stream with minimal effort.

But now Frank was thinking of a different problem. What to do about his clothes. As the morning light began to shine, Frank knew it would be a sunny day because of his observing the night skies without clouds, allowing him to gaze up at the stars.   Frank again exited the stream and put his pants back on. He found a secluded area where he could rest and let the morning sun dry his clothes. He did take off his shoes and prop them up where sunshine could enter the shoes to help them to dry. Tired from the vigor and stress of his ordeal, he fell asleep. All he wanted was a short "Cat Nap" but he slept for several hours. When he awoke, his clothes were almost dry. But his shoes were still very damp.

Frank moved along the edge of the wooded area where he had slept and looked for any signs of life. There was more traffic moving along the road that still paralleled the stream. Frank would walk North, staying close to the undergrowth and wooded area along the stream to hide when he saw cars and trucks getting near on the roadway. He did not want to be seen walking close to the stream and raise suspicions. He passed several houses and small farms along the way. There were occasional dogs around the houses that would bark at Frank even though he was some distance from them. Once a barking dog got the attention of his master, but the dog's bark was followed by a sharp rebuke of byt zticha (shut up!). It seemed that the dog's concerns were not his owner's concerns.

Now Frank passed a house where a woman was hanging her wash on a line to dry in the morning sun. Frank paused to watch her as she went about one of her daily chores. Soon the wash was hung and Frank noticed that there were several pairs of pants along with some shirts that she had hung up. Immediately the thought came to him about stealing a pair of pants and a shirt so that he could shuck himself of the military garments he wore. Just as soon as the thought entered his mind, Frank remembered the commandment "Thou shalt not steal."

Frank wrestled within his mind of what to do. He knew that to take a pair of pants and a shirt that was not his was a sin. Yet how was he going to be able to move about Hamburg in the clothes he wore? If he did not rid himself of them, he would most certainly be found out and returned to the military camp. What to do, what to do. How can you justify theft, or can you? Does the end result justify the means by which you get there? It was a moral dilemma for Frank, one he had not encountered with consequences of this magnitude before. Frank decided that it was imperative that he return to his family in the States and not spend six years in the military. So, the decision was made, he would remain hidden in the underbrush until he thought the clothes had ample time to dry, then bolt out and grab a pair of pants and a shirt and then make it back to the underbrush, hoping he would not be seen. But he could not wait too long or the lady may come back out to take her laundry in, then Frank's opportunity would be gone!

He knew that he must find other clothes. He prayed for forgiveness for the sin he was about to commit. Was this act going to be a sin of presumptiveness on Frank's part, presuming on the mercies of God? After praying and waiting and praying and waiting, he thought the clothes on the line must be almost dry. Frank approached the clothes line where some sheets on the line blocked the view from the house. Then he thought, "What if they have a dog?" The dog would sense his presence and sound the alarm. He prayed there would be no dog. There was not. Frank quickly grabbed a shirt and a pair of pants that appeared to be about his size and just as quickly returned to the wooded area along the stream.

Frank changed into the clothes he had just stolen and again asked God for forgiveness. He tied a knot in the end of the shirt sleeves and pants legs. Looking around for stones to place in them, he found none, so he filled the legs and sleeves with dirt and then cast them into the stream. They sank quickly, now if they would only stay sunk for enough time to allow Frank to get to Hamburg and find a way home.

Onward! On towards Hamburg. Frank occupied his mind wondering how he would be able to board a ship once he got to Hamburg. With no passport, he could not buy a ticket even if he had the money, which he did not. Without a ticket he could not obtain a boarding pass. Most of the day Frank walked and walked toward Hamburg, staying within the brush and wood line of the stream to go unnoticed. No breakfast. No lunch. Frank's hunger began to nag on him, making his stomach growl like a puppy tugging at a rag in play. But this was not play, it was for real.

Continuing his trek, Frank noticed an elderly farmer harvesting vegetables from his small garden and loading them on a dilapidated looking old truck. Walking up to him, Frank asked if he needed any help harvesting the vegetables. The man looked around with a quizzical stare as if he was wondering, "Where did he come from?" He then answered yes, but he could not pay for any hired help. Frank said he would be glad to help in exchange for some food to eat. The man replied in the affirmative so Frank pitched in as though he knew what to do without instructions, and he did know what to do. He had had ample experience on the small plotnic that his parents owned before migrating to America, plus what he had learned working on a truck farm in Texas as he grew up.

As they had gone about harvesting and loading the vegetables, they engaged in small talk, all in German. Frank learned that he was a widower with no children and that he lived alone on that small piece of land. He raised vegetables and took them to market to earn a meager living. It was enough to buy him the necessities of life plus some occasional meat. He also traded vegetables to nearby farmers for pork. The old farmer also had a few chickens which he raised for meat and eggs. He also supplemented his diet with an occasional catfish from the stream below.

Frank knew about catfish too. He and his father had set lines out on the Brazos River in Texas and caught many catfish. In exchanging fish stories, Frank had let the information slip out about catfish in Texas on the Brazos River. Inquisitively, the man had asked where Texas was as he did not know and was not familiar with the United States of America.

The two of them developed a kindred friendship almost instantaneously. The old man seemed to see in Frank the son he had never had. For Frank, the old man brought back memories of his father who had now passed on. It was good to get his hands back into the soil. Next to freshly sawn wood and the smell of sawdust, Frank loved the smell of good, rich earth. Plus, it brought back memories of his youth when he helped his own father gather vegetables from their garden. But this garden was much larger. Soon the back of the old truck was filled with cabbages and potatoes. It was beginning to grow dark as evening began to bear down on them.

After the last of the garden was loaded, the old man said with a satisfied smile, "Now let us eat."

They walked back to the modest house, stopping at the well where the each took turns pumping water for the other to wash their hands. The water was colder than the stream! That is because it came from deep in the ground. Cool, fresh water. What a blessing Frank thought. Secretly under his breath Frank thanked the Lord for the blessings he enjoyed, even during the ordeal he had been through. And the ones he had yet to face.

The inside of the house was modestly furnished. Much of the furniture was simple, but adequate, the kitchen table appeared to be hand-made. It was put together quite well and had the sturdiness of one carved from solid rock. The house had the wonderful warmth and aroma that only a wood burning stove can give a house!

The old man gave directions and Frank began to cut up a cabbage brought in from the garden. Meanwhile, the old man put some wood in his stove, along with some corn cobs and small kindling and lit the fire. Then he began to slice up a portion of sausage into a large pan. He added some butter and placed it on top of the wood burning stove's open port after removing the metal plate covering it. He directed Frank to place the cut cabbage on top of the sausage in the pan. Adding a little water, salt, pepper, a small amount of onion left over from something, and some garlic. The preparation was done, now it just had to cook until the cabbage was tender. It soon began to simmer so the old man covered the pan with a lid so that I would build up steam in the pan and help cook the cabbage as the sausage sizzled on the bottom of the pan and furnished flavor from the fat and suet.

They served themselves portions of the cabbage and sausage from the pan. At the table the old man bowed his head to say grace. "Thank you, God, for this food from your bounty. Thank you for my new friend, Frank. I also ask your blessings on the trip to market and to help in the selling of these vegetables which we harvested this morning. I ask in Jesus' Holy Name. Amen."

Frank joined in saying amen to that prayer.

"So, you have lived in America," the man asked as they ate their meal. "You speak good German but with a slight Czech accent," he continued.

Frank sensed that he could trust the old man with information about his circumstances. Frank explained that he was born in Kunvald in what is now the Czech Republic but was the Austria-Hungarian empire when he had left. He had learned both Czech and German as a child. He explained that he was 10 years old when his family moved to America and settled in one of its states named Texas. There, Frank's father worked in a cotton gin for a while and then on a cotton farm for a time and later went into carpentry. Frank grew up doing carpenter work with his dad and was quite proficient in the trade having served an apprenticeship under his father's tutelage. He also told him that he had wanted to return to his homeland in Czechoslovakia as nostalgia tugged at his heart to visit the old home place, if it was still standing, and to re-acquaint himself with some of his boyhood friends, if they could be found.

"What year did your family leave Czechoslovakia?" the man asked.

"1901" Frank replied, "Just at the end turning of the new century."

"Why did you return?" the man asked, even though Frank had already mentioned that.

"Something inside of me kept me longing to see the old home place," Frank said. "I suppose it was to re-affirm that moving to America was the correct choice that my father had made," he explained. "And it was to see how things had faired with my friends of that long ago time. To see if they were well and what had happened to them."

In a way, Frank was making the journey to Kunvald trying to evaluate what his life and circumstances would be like if the family had not moved to America. He supposed that it would have turned out similar to what his friends had encountered. Whatever it was, Frank had a deep longing to see the homeland. One he could not fully explain.

"I did not realize the political situation was such as it is," Frank continued, "or I would not have come at this time."

"I am afraid that Germany is going to go to war with Czechoslovakia," the old man stated. "Germany wants the Sudetenland. They say it should be part of Germany, but Czechoslovakia does not want to part with it because in that northern part of the Czech Republic is most of the heavy manufacturing that adds to the Czech economy."

From the man's conversation Frank surmised that he had traveled far enough in the stream that he was now in Germany. It was a relief to Frank, maybe any search for him would stop at the border. A sense of relative safety came over Frank, even though he realized he was still in dire circumstances.

"Where are you traveling too?" the old man asked of Frank as if he had not heard Frank's first answer.

Frank replied, "To Hamburg for passage back to America where I have a wife and daughter and a small piece of land." Frank did not believe that the old man suffered from memory problems, perhaps he was just checking the consistency of Frank's odyssey to determine the truthfulness of Frank's tale.

"You are traveling light," the old man said. "You must have not planned on spending much time in Kunvald with no suitcase or change of clothes."

Frank marveled at the astuteness of the old man; he was very observant. Letting his guard down, Frank related the story of how his suitcase was taken. Frank opened his innermost thoughts to the old man and told him of his being conscripted into military service as a Czech citizen. How he had escaped and how he had traveled thus far on his trek to Hamburg. How he was trying to make it back to America to his wife and young daughter. The old man listened quietly as he ate.

When Frank had finished, the old man said, "You can ride in my truck to market if you wish, I am going to go to Hamburg in the morning to sell vegetables. Most of the time I sell locally, but on occasion I go to Hamburg where the city folks seem more appreciative and generous to get fresh vegetables. It is a little further but I am usually rewarded with better prices. So tomorrow I think I will take my goods to Hamburg."

Frank realized the old man was doing this on this day just to help him out on his journey.

"I am very much appreciative," Frank said as he thanked the man for his courtesy. "It means very much to me" he continued. "I will help you unload when we get there."

"There is no unloading, everyone sells off the back of his truck, unless you sell the whole load to one of the dealers there. But I do not do that as you get less money for your goods," the old man told Frank.

After finishing their meal, they cleaned up and washed the few dishes and the pan that they had used. The old man showed Frank the spare quest room which had been unused for years upon years. They engaged in small talk about things in general along with their hopes and dreams for the future. Frank had already mentioned that he had a small piece of land and said he had a cow which provided milk and butter. One of Frank's dreams was to one day buy a second cow. As the day was coming to an end, they went to bed, Frank on a goose down featherbed in the guest room and the old man in his own room. As Frank lay on the bed, his mind rehearsed the events of the day and pondered the conversations he had had with the old man. Frank noticed that the old man had not said anything political, no criticism of the German government, or about the elected and appointed officials, or the means and ways in which they governed. Yet it was obvious to Frank that the old man was dissatisfied with the status quo. "Why do I think that," Frank wondered, yet he could not identify the reason for that impression. Perhaps it was his tone and mannerisms when he had talked about Germany wanting to acquire the Sudetenland from Czechoslovakia. It seemed the old man was against the idea, though he was careful not to say so openly.

Morning seemed to come quickly. Mainly because they had gone to bed late and woke up very early, as was his custom. It was still dark outside when the old man woke Frank and told him to get up through the closed door. Frank had slept soundly, being very tired from his journey thus far. Plus, it had been a long time since he had stooped over and over harvesting vegetables. His back ached and his arms were sore.

They both worked in unison to cook breakfast. Fresh eggs from the man's chicken pen, scrambled to perfection. Thick slices of home smoked bacon. Homemade bread like Frank's mother used to bake. Frank thought of those days when his mother baked bread. The house would be filled with the wonderful, delicious smell of fresh bread. Frank always liked the first slice, or the last slice best, the "heels" as they called them. That way he had one side of that wonderful crust and the other side on which to smear large helpings of home churned butter to melt down into the fresh hot bread.

Thinking about how the old man used dry corn cobs to help start the fire reminded him of his mother cooking on a wood stove. She had a knack for knowing just how many corn cobs were needed to bake with. There was no temperature gauge on the stove, but his mother had learned over time how many cobs were needed to bake bread, how many for kolaches, how many for boiling water and other cooking needs. How she did it he did not know.

After breakfast, the old man and Frank cleaned up again, putting everything back into its assigned place. Then, going outside, they climbed into the old truck. It was still dark. Frank had no idea of what time it was, though he knew it was early. There were no clocks in the house or timepieces of any sort to tell time with, the old man just did everything by his internal time clock. Frank commented on the fact that the old man did not have any clocks, and asked what time it was.

"Don't need a clock or time piece," the old man said. "Day follows day, and night follows night. I wake early and do all I can during the day. Eat when I am hungry and sleep when I am tired. God takes care of the rest," the old man said. It was a simple but very adequate philosophy of life, Frank thought.

The trip to Hamburg began with a loud backfire, as if the truck resented being put to work that early in the morning. The truck was bouncy and smoked a little. Settling down into the well-worn, broken springs passenger seat, Frank wondered if it would make it to Hamburg. Almost as if the old man was reading Frank's mind, he said, "Do not worry, old Anna here may seem like it is falling apart but we have made this trip many times with no problems."

They pulled out of the man's homestead and onto the highway. It was a bright, clear morning with the Sun shining brightly. Birds were singing as though they were ushering them on their way. Frank wondered how many people failed to appreciate the small things in life that seem to go unnoticed. Fresh vegetables, homemade bread, hand sliced bacon, the songs of the many birds that abound everywhere. A nice clear day with a gently breeze. The smell of wood burning in stoves along the way, with chimneys of houses sending streams of woody smoke into the air. Wild flowers opening their petals to welcome the morning sun as someone stretches out their arms to welcome a friend or relative from an absence. New friends, good memories. Small things. But so wonderful.

The old man and Frank completed the journey in small talk. The Hamburg open air market was on the South side, and they circled the square looking for suitable place to park. The center of the square was filled with empty tables. The old man spotted a space and carefully backed his open bed stake truck into the slot. Soon there were no more parking spaces left. Those late-comers who were not so fortunate as to find a parking space had to park elsewhere and carry their goods to the open tables, which they had to pay extra for.

Frank lingered around the truck and the old man, not wanting to part company. But he knew that he had to get to the harbor and figure out a way to get aboard one of the passenger ships. Saying goodbye was hard, even though they had only known each other for about a day, yet a connection was made that is hard to sever. Frank and the old man knew the parting would be forever; they would never see each other again. Frank committed the old man's name and mailing address to memory. Frank did not want to write it down in case something happened to him, he did not want the old man implicated in any way by having his name and address on him.

Saying goodbye, Frank started walking through the more industrialized part of Hamburg towards the harbor. He strolled around until he located the Harbormaster's Office. Outside the office there was a list of the arriving and departing ships posted on a crude bulletin board. Only one ship was leaving for America today, and that was scheduled to depart in about 3 hours. No arrivals for the next several days from America, so it would be that time plus a few days for ships to be refitted for the return trips again. Frank decided this was going to have to be the one. He could not take a chance on loitering around Hamburg for up to a week.

Walking around the port, he located the ship. It was a three stacker. It looked sharp and clean as if it had just been repainted. Mooring lines stretched from the bow, stern, and leeward side. There was no way Frank could scale those lines without being spotted, it would take too long and the chance of additional activity that might arise around the dock made it an impossible means of boarding. The boarding passengers were going up the ramp and onto the deck, but only after having their papers and boarding pass checked by two German uniformed military guards manning either side of the gang plank.

Looking around for crews that may be loading the ship with supplies for the trip to America, he noticed they were all wearing clearly identified clothing. They were members of a guild and they protected their occupation ferociously. Frank realized there was no way of joining in the crews that were loading the ship. There must be some other way Frank thought. He pondered the situation, trying to come up with an alternative plan. There was none.

Frank waited and waited as passenger after passenger had their papers checked and proceeded up the gangplank. The line was dwindling rapidly and soon was only a trickle, then just an occasional passenger rushing to make it onboard on time. Finally, a "Last Call" was made and Frank watched as the last border had passed the checkpoint.

Desperate, Frank prayed "Lord Jesus, you opened blind eyes when you were here among us, I pray Lord that you blind these eyes that can see so that I might board this ship, I am depending on you Lord, you are my only hope at this point. I have no other way unless you make a way." With that Frank summoned up all the courage he had and began walking toward the boarding guards. He dared not catch their gaze or look directly at them, but focusing his attention on the top of the gangplank he kept walking straight ahead.

As he drew closer and closer to the guards, his heart beat faster and faster. His heart beat also seemed louder and louder, as Frank felt the blood pulsing in his body. It seemed to him that it was so loud that if the guards did not see him, they would most certainly hear his heart pounding in his chest. Onward he walked. He walked right between the guards as if they were not even there! They did not make a move until Frank was at the top of the gangplank and on board the ship. As soon as Frank was onboard, the guards started backing the gang plank away! Frank marveled at what he deemed to be a miracle worked by God! A miracle that only God could do!

Walking around the ship until he was on the opposite side from the dock, Frank looked out on the Elbe and gave thanks to God for answered prayer. After the ship had cast off, Frank mingled with the other passengers on deck as they waved to loved ones on the pier as the ship slipped further and further away. Having learned a lesson about the clothes he wore, Frank analyzed what everyone else was wearing. It was not long before he felt that he fit in more with the second class or steerage class of passengers and so he migrated below deck with them.

Walking around in the steerage section, he looked for an unoccupied berth in which to sleep. He thought it best to spot several and wait until everyone had turned in so that he did not inadvertently get someone else's spot and cause a ruckus that would bring attention to him. Finding none he ventured up on deck where many passengers were still taking in the sights along the Elbe. Frank was looking for an indiscreet place to spend the night. That is when he noticed the lifeboats with canvas covers laced across them. That was an idea; perhaps he could manage to get into one of the lifeboats and remain unseen.

He found a lifeboat away from the crowd and pretended to be looking out at the sights. But he was really observing the rope that laced around the canvas cover on the boat to discover how best to get it undone. The main tiedown was at the bow of the boat and was a slip knot so it could be easily undone and the canvas removed in the event of an emergency. This would be the one, Frank thought.

He spent his day meandering about the ship. At meal time he went through the cafeteria line in the steerage section.   Then more strolling the ship, being careful to avoid any of the ship's officers. Frank passed the lifeboat he planned to sleep in. There was always the chance he could find some spot in steerage to sleep, but a greater chance of being discovered or turned in by the other passengers. On one such trip around the deck Frank was chased off the poop deck (the stern area of the ship above the first-class section). Only first-class passengers were allowed access to that area. Even though Frank was first class in his attitude and demeanor on the inside, he certainly did not appear so on the outside by his attire. One of the ship's officers gave Frank a stern admonition to stay away from first class areas of the ship.

Once, when no one was around, Frank took a cushion from a deck chair and slipped it under the canvas covering the life boat that he had loosened the ties on. The fact that the ties were still loose gave evidence that the untied end of the canvas had not been noticed and re-tied. Frank thought he could use the cushion as a pillow.

Eating was not a problem. Frank would blend in with the crowd moving through the cafeteria line and get what he wanted to eat. Not that there was much choice, it was still mostly boiled potatoes or cabbage, and boiled stringy beef. And bread. Mostly dried bread. Things had not changed much from Frank's first trip on the way to America. For a moment he pondered the possibility of following one of the stewards serving the First-Class section to locate the ship's laundry. He thought about the possibility of getting a steward's clothes that may be tossed into a laundry hamper for washing. Then he could help clean the tables and get some scraps of food from the leftovers that would be carried to the kitchen and dumped. It was too risky, he thought and abandoned the idea.

At the end of the day, when darkness prevailed, Frank would stand on the deck next to the life boat and slowly loosen the canvas further. When he had it sufficiently open for him to slip inside, he would stand in front of the prepared opening with his back to it to shield it from sight while he made sure there were no other persons around that might observe his activities. He would pretend to be looking at the upper reaches of the ship and the dark smoke streaming up and backward from the stacks. When Frank had assured himself that no one was around, he pulled himself up on the bulwark of the life boat and slipped inside. Once inside he tried to arrange the open canvas back to its original position to help conceal what he had done.

Frank was an early riser and was usually awake before daybreak. He would listen for footsteps on the deck and for voices of people talking. When all was quiet, he would slip out of the life boat and onto the ship's deck. Putting the canvas back in order, he would then navigate below deck for breakfast. Breakfast was not much better than the other meals. The coffee was terrible. Once Frank saw them making coffee. The cook, or most likely one of the kitchen help, would dump ground coffee into a big kettle and then pour hot water on top of the grounds. After it sat for a few minutes, one could dispense coffee through the spigot at the bottom.

It was the same routine, day after day, meal after meal. Until one day, the fifth day at sea, when Frank was exiting the lifeboat a ship's officer exited one of the main doors from the main body of the ship to the deck at precisely the same time Frank was exiting the lifeboat! The ship's officer immediately blew a brass whistle he had hung around his neck with three sharp, loud blasts. Immediately, as if out of nowhere, other ship's officers appeared and Frank was caught. A stowaway. For the first time in his life Frank felt the cold steel of handcuffs as they clicked around his wrists. He was asked for a boarding pass permit. None. He was asked for a passport identification. None. He was asked for any form of identification. None. All the while Frank was trying to explain why he did not have a passport, boarding pass, or identification. There were no ears to hear. Frank later surmised the three blows on the whistle was some sort of standard call for help.

He was escorted to a holding cell, which was more like a stark cabin with only a bed and toilet. It locked and unlocked from the outside. No porthole. But Frank could not fit through a porthole, and even if he could, where would he go? There was no place to escape to! He took comfort in the fact that the ship would not turn around on his account but would proceed to the its appointed destination, New York. At that point he would have more opportunity to plead his case when they arrived in port.   At least he had a more comfortable sleeping arrangement! And better food, he hoped, that he did not have to stand in line for.

The ship made port in New York. The old Castle Garden dock and immigration center had given way to newer facilities in Manhattan. Most passengers were then ferried to Ellis Island for processing as Ellis Island was too shallow to provide docking facilities. It was on one of these ferry trips that Frank was escorted to Ellis Island and reported to the proper authorities.

Having no identification, Frank identified himself as Frank Vancik, who was born in Kunvald, Austria-Hungary, which is now the present-day Czech Republic. Frank rehearsed his story over and over to the various officials, telling how he wanted to visit his homeland and the events that transpired after reaching Czechoslovakia.   It was determined to turn Frank over to the representatives of the Czech Republic.   Frank was escorted to another holding cell within the Ellis Island processing station.

The next day Frank was taken from the cell and brought before what appeared to be a tribunal. Frank was seated in front of a long table behind which sat various official-looking people. He thought they were officials as they all wore suits and ties. Some had nameplates in front of them, but the writing was so small Frank could not read it from where he sat. One of the men started asking questions to which Frank responded, retelling his story, how he came to the United States in 1901 with his father and mother. That he had lived continuously in the U.S. since 1901. That he was married and had a two-year-old daughter living in Rosenberg, Texas. But he had no proof of all his explanations.

He was turned over to the authority of Czech immigration officials and, under their purview, returned to his cell. On the way back to his confinement, Frank asked one of the guards, "What will happen now?"

The answer sent chills down Frank's spine. "You will be returned to the Czech Republic and be shot as a deserter" the guard said with a laugh in his voice that represented his delight in Frank's misfortune. How can this be, he wondered. Is there no balm in Gilead? There must be some higher authority to which he could appeal. The American Embassy! That is what he would do, appeal to the American Embassy. But the embassy official seemed to have meager interest in Frank's case since he was not a U.S. citizen and turned a deaf ear to Frank's pleading.

Frank paced back and forth across his cell. He felt like a caged animal and wondered if that was the same feeling that animals in the zoo felt. Once free to roam and do whatever they wanted without restriction, to be suddenly captured and confined to a cage. Frank resolved never to feel the same toward animals in the zoo after this. That is, if there were an "after this."

Later that day Frank overheard a conversation between two professionally dressed gentlemen and a prisoner across the cell from Frank's. Frank seemed to hear that they were reporters for a newspaper in New York.

As their conversation ended, Frank called out to them, "Sir, sir," he stated, "Are you newspaper men?" he asked.

"Yes" came the reply.

"I must speak with you," Frank pleaded.

"What about?" one of the men asked.

Frank related his case to them as they listened intently. Frank said he had nowhere else to go or turn to, perhaps they could get a message to his wife in Texas and she could come to New York and vouch for him. That he has been living in the United States since the age of 10, that he is married to a US citizen and has a daughter who is a citizen by birth. Frank illustrated that his case was desperate as he was to be returned to Europe and shot. His life depended on them getting a message to his wife.

The men listened intently but took no notes. Frank asked for a piece of paper and pencil to write down his address in Texas for them. Having been given a page from one of their note pads they carried, Frank recorded the contact information for his wife, and once again pleaded with them to get in touch with her and explain his situation.

Days past.

Then one of the reporters that Frank had talked to asked the other, "Did you ever do a follow up on that fellow that told us he was living in Texas and to get in touch with his wife?"

"No, I thought you had," the other replied.

Then the first reporter said, "Why don't we give a call to our affiliate in Houston and have them check it out?"

"Okay, good idea," the other reporter said as he rummaged through papers and notes on his desk and located the information Frank had given him. Picking up the phone and looking up the number, he called Houston. The contact in Houston expressed great interest in this story. Having relayed the information to them, he put the phone down and continued with other duties.

In Houston, the story was related to the press manager. A slip of paper with the name and address he took over the phone from New York was handed to him.

"There might be a story here," he said as he gave the slip of paper back to the reporter who gave it to him. "Take one of the company cars and drive down to Rosenberg and check it out, should only take a couple hours, an hour down there and an hour back plus looking up the address," he said.

Armed with permission, the reporter headed for the parking lot after getting the keys to a press vehicle from the front desk. As the manager had predicted, it was about an hour's drive to Rosenberg. Once there he went to the county courthouse and looked for any records or tax bills in the name of Frank Vancik. To his surprise, there was a property tax statement in Frank's name. The address matched the address given him over the phone from New York.

Next, he acquired a map of Rosenberg and located the address. It was just outside the city limits but only a short drive. Arriving at the modest dwelling, he knocked on the door. Frank's wife was behind the house feeding chickens but had seen the car drive up to the house.

She was walking around to the front of the house as the man was beginning to step back off the front porch, she asked, "May I help you?"

"Yes," the man stated, "Are you Bosinia Vancik?" he asked.

"Yes" she replied.

"I have come to give you information on your husband, Frank," he said.

"He is not here, he went to Czechoslovakia to see his birth place and some friends and relatives there but should have been back already," she said.

"That is why I came to see you. My office in Houston received a call from our New York affiliate and told us that your husband is in confinement at Ellis Island and is about to be sent back to the Czech Republic where he will be shot as a deserter. He got a message to two of our reporters in New York to relay to you that he needs you to come to New York and vouch for him," the reporter said.

Bosinia was stunned by this information. "But he has a passport! And how can he be a deserter when he has never been in the military?" Bosinia asked. Her expression bespoke "I told him not to go" along with bewilderment and confusion as to how this situation came about. Never the less, it was now up to her to save her husband. A myriad of thoughts swirled around in her mind. She tried to sort them out but nothing made sense. All she knew was that she had to get to Ellis Island, and quickly.

After the man left, she went to the kitchen and opened one of the canisters and began to count out how much money she and Frank had stowed away. They did not trust banks and kept all their funds in one of the kitchen canisters. As she unfolded the bills and sorted them into stacks, she began to think that there was not enough money. Panic set in. How could she get more money? What could she sell? The house they were buying, the cow, some jewelry? What? What? She told herself to remain calm and start praying, that through prayer all things can work out.

She contacted the train station in Houston to inquire about a train ticket to New York. She learned that she had just enough money in the canister for a round-trip ticket for herself and her daughter. Then she called the Greyhound bus line to inquire about tickets to New York. The bus was less expensive, which would allow for any incidentals along the way, it would be more comfortable too, as the train only offered wooden benches. At the ticket price she was quoted from the agent at the bus station, she could afford the ticket, it was less than a train ticket. But it would necessitate the changing of buses several times as there was no direct bus lines to New York. A train ticket with sleeping arrangements was much more expensive. By bus it would be.

But what about Frank? He would need a ticket to come home. Then there was the fare to get to Houston to catch an earlier bus that did not pass through Rosenberg, unless a neighbor drove her, and then there would be a fare to get from the bus station in New York, which was at the Port Authority in New York. Then the ferry to Ellis Island. There were so many unknowns. How soon after getting to New York would they be able to go to Ellis Island? Would they need hotel accommodations? How much was food going to cost? She thought she needed extra money "just in case" to overcome obstacles on the way. It would be better to have too much than not enough. Frank's life was at stake and that meant more to her than all the "things" she might have to sell.

Since the trip by bus would take almost all of two days, she had to plan. What would they need for the trip, there and back? What documents should she take? Since Bosinia and Emilie were both born in the United States, a birth certificate would prove citizenship. She also packed her and Frank's marriage license. Glancing at the marriage certificate, she noticed the date of 1911. How much had transpired between when they were first married and now? They made it through tough times before and they would make it through this as well, she thought. She packed some tax statements showing their address in Rosenberg. Also, a copy of their Federal Income tax return for last year, 1921. She placed all the documents in one large brown envelope and all her money in another and buried both at the bottom of her handbag.

Her parents and Frank's parents were both gone so they could not help. They had no brothers or sisters, only their two-year-old daughter who could not grow up without a father! In desperation she contacted the bank that held the mortgage on the small piece of land and house that they had. The banker's only suggestion was to sell the house. There was a moderate demand for houses in that area, so she contacted a real estate company and to list the house for quick sale, she even told them she would consider offers. Then she was informed that Texas is a community property state and she could not sell the house without her husband's signature! Selling the house was out. Things were looking bleaker and bleaker.

As a last resort, she pulled some jewelry out of her jewelry box. It was things she did not wear as they were keepsakes from her mother, who had gotten them from her mother. A gold necklace with a large piece of green glass as the main setting with earrings to match. At least all she thought of the necklace is that it had a large piece of what she thought to be "Green Glass" but was a large emerald! They were too fancy for her to wear anyway, she thought, besides, I do not have anything to wear with them. And we never go to places where such fancy things are worn. Even though she had a sentimental attachment to them, she took them to a local jeweler and asked their worth. She did not expect very much. She described them to the jeweler who then examined them with a small microscope, clinched over one eye.

"These are nice pieces," he said. "They have old world workmanship that is not often seen today. The green glass setting you described is an emerald." He then offered her a substantial sum for them. She was astounded! She took it!

Next the cow, the cow was easy to sell. Then the chickens. All that was left was Frank's carpenter tools and some household belongings. The tools sold quickly. The household belongings were able to be left in place since the house would not be sold, the clothes, dishes, cookware, and such could stay in place. They would not bring much anyway, she thought. She counted her money again and was satisfied that she had enough. Besides, there was nothing left to sell. Whatever she had, it would have to do!

A neighbor agreed to drive her and her daughter to Houston to the bus station.

"Where are we going Momma?" young Emilie asked.

"To see Papa and bring him home," she responded.

Bosinia and Emilie loaded up into the neighbor's car with a suitcase of necessities along with a change of clothes; for themselves and a change of clothes for Frank. With that being done, they headed for Houston and a world of unknowns. As they traveled along, the adults were discussing the situation. Young Emilie in the backseat could overhear enough to get a grasp on the seriousness of her father's predicament. She began to cry softly, trying not to let the adults know, but they did. Bosinia turned and comforted Emilie the best she could.

"Now do not worry, Emilie, "she said, "all things work out, we just have to put our trust and faith in God."

Turning back around she put a finger to her lips while looking at her neighbor as if to say "Shush, let's change the subject." Then she immediately began commenting on such a nice car her neighbor had and what a beautiful day it was.

Arriving at the station, she thanked her neighbor for driving them to the bus station, then she went inside and purchased a round-trip ticket for two to New York. Asking directions to which bus they should board, It was pointed out to them. They had about an hour before the bus left, but too long to board at the present time, so they found some benches to sit on while they listened for boarding instructions for their bus to be announced.

Emilie's eyes scanned everything in the building in a sense of wonder. Just as she had done looking out the window of the car on the way to Houston. It was her first trip that she could remember and certainly the largest city she had ever seen, and the biggest building she had ever been in. She wondered how they were able to build buildings so tall. And all the noise of the city, it certainly was not like Rosenberg!

Soon the bus call came and they both boarded the bus, filled with anxiety, coupled, and compounded with stress. Would her suitcase make it to New York with them, what if they put it on the wrong bus? What if? What if? Bo's mind was full of "what ifs." The air inside the bus smelt like the diesel exhaust emitted by the many buses in the station that were idling between departures. She hoped it would clear out once they were traveling the highway. And it did.

The estimated travel time was one day and eighteen hours. Plus, the day in preparation, that would make almost three days since she first got word of Frank's plight before she would have a chance to see him. Before the newspaper man left, who had brought her the news, she asked him to relay information back to Frank that she would be on the way as soon as possible and how long it may take.

For Frank time seemed like a double-edged sword. On the one hand, time crept slowly along, minutes seemed like hours and hours like days. Yet on the other hand, his time was running out as the day of his deportation seemed to be streaking toward him like a meteor. He wondered constantly if his message got through to Bo. What if it did not?

Frank got the news the next day and was told the trip would last almost two days. That means Frank would have to circumvent being deported for at least two more days, maybe three. He was worried, what if there were delays for one reason or another, and Bo arrived a day late! A day after he had been deported, and the ship would not turn around to bring him back. Then what would he do when he landed at Hamburg again and was turned over to the authorities there?

After what seemed a lifetime, the bus finally arrived in New York. Almost two days of riding made one's body felt sore all over. Fortunately, the bus drivers had to change shifts at various stations along the way. This allowed Bo and Emilie to get off the bus for a brief time to stretch their legs and get something simple to eat at the concession. Whatever they got had to be eaten in the station as no food or beverage were allowed on the bus. If the announcement was made to reboard the bus, one had to leave unconsumed food and beverages behind or miss the bus and must wait for the next one. Bo and Emilie ate in a hurry to avoid such a mishap in timing that would delay their trip that much longer.

In New York, the bus pulled into the station known as the Port Authority. It was very near the ferry to Ellis Island. When Bo and Emilie exited the bus, they were surprised to be met by officials from the United States State Department. They had been alerted by the newspaper reporters to be looking for a single female passenger with a two-year-old daughter and had been given their names. They were easy to spot. The officials welcomed them to New York and explained how they had been contacted concerning Frank's plight. The State Department took a renewed interest in Frank's case since he was married to a US citizen.

It was 10 AM when the bus arrived at the station. The State Department had already been in touch with Ellis Island Immigration and learned that Frank was scheduled to be deported on a ship leaving for Hamburg at 3 PM that same day. That left only about 5 hours for Bo and Emilie to get their suitcase which had not yet been unloaded! And make it to Ellis Island. It seemed forever before Bo saw her suitcase being placed on a luggage cart. The wait was almost unbearable. Time seems to slow down when you are facing a crisis and every minute counts.

Finally retrieving her luggage, the State Department officials escorted her and Emilie to a waiting car and took them to the ferry. Thankfully, once across to Ellis Island the officials knew exactly where to go. Bo and Emilie were told to have a seat in a waiting area while the US officials tried to resolve the situation. They were meeting with immigration officials from the US and some other important looking men. They engaged in conversation that Bo could not hear, but the conversation escalated loudly into almost an argument. Then one of the US officials came back to where Bo and Emilie sat and asked for her birth certificate, marriage certificate, seeing the IRS tax form, he asked for that as well.

Going back to the conversation, he showed the papers to the other individuals and each took turns in looking them over. Finally, word was sent to bring Frank into the room. Once he arrived, and he saw Bo and Emilie in the waiting area, his countenance seemed to brighten and a smile came across his face. Frank explained the entire episode again, how his passport was taken and he was sentenced to serve 6 years in the military as a citizen of the Czech Republic, though it was Austria-Hungary when Frank immigrated to the US with his parents at the age of ten.

After what seemed to be another half an hour of bickering and arguing, Frank was told to rejoin his family....he was free to enter the United States and go home to Texas. He tried to walk to Bo and Emilie but it was a quick step that grew faster and faster until it broke into a run to Bo's arms. Frank, Bo, and Emilie embraced for a long time with Frank showering them both with kisses. Free to go to Texas, what a relief! Suddenly tiredness swept over them all with the release of stress and the tenseness of the past days resolved. Much thanks and appreciation were given to the officials from the Department of State who acquired Frank's release and restoration to his family.

Frank and family ferried to Manhattan, and, after taking stock of how much money they had left, checked into a hotel to spend time together, catch up on all the events and to gain some much-needed rest. Calling from the hotel, they learned that the first bus to depart for Houston would be at 8 a.m. in the morning. The next one after that would be noon. They decided to get the 8 a.m. bus so they could be back in Texas all the sooner.

That evening at the hotel was a time of celebration and reunion. Frank recounted his ordeal and to the miraculous providence of God in sustaining him and comforting him. How he walked between the guards to get on the ship after the prayer he uttered was most miraculous of all. As tired as they all were, it was difficult to sleep that night. Waking early in the morning, they were going to hail a taxi to take them to the bus station but the doorman intervened. He explained how they could get a courtesy ride to the bus station from the hotel car reserved for such occasions. In doing so, they saved the taxi fare, which was much appreciated and represented by the gratuity they gave the doorman out of the savings his information provided.

At the bus station Frank purchased a one-way ticket to Houston as Bo and Emilie had previously purchased a round-trip ticket. There was a two hour wait for the next available bus. During those two hours they took a short walk to see more of the city and to look out across the water at Ellis Island and the Statue of Liberty. They were always careful not to stray too far from the bus station, however, as they did not want to get lost or meander so far away, they could not get back to the station in time.

Frank had written a letter to the old man in Germany to let him know he had made it safely and was united with his family. At the bus station he tore it up and disposed of it in a trash can. He reasoned that if it were discovered or intercepted by the authorities it would bring trouble to the old man who so graciously helped him. Yet he wanted to convey the message to the old man. Frank had a sudden inspiration. He bought a postcard at the bus station concession that portrayed the Statue of Liberty. In the message section of the card, he wrote only two words: "Two Cows." He purchased postage on it and dropped it in the outgoing mail box. Frank knew that the old man would know what it meant!

The announcement to board the bus for Houston was made and it was now time to board. The bus had two seats on either side of the center aisle. Deciding who would sit where was resolved when it was agreed that at every stop to change drivers, they would exchange seats, for the person who was alone would sit next to a papa until the next change. Frank said he would start the journey next to Bo and then it would be Emilie's turn to sit next to her papa.

A day and eighteen hours later, they expected to be in Houston. They calculated they would arrive in Houston during daylight hours. The trip was as tiring as was the trip to New York. Each dozed off to sleep from time to time, especially in the night time. Next, they had to determine how they would get to their home from Houston. They might call one of their neighbors whom they knew had a phone. When they did arrive in Houston, they discovered that they could catch a bus from Houston to San Antonio, which made a stop in Rosenberg. Perfect. No need to have a neighbor drive all the way to Houston!

Arriving in Rosenberg, they then called upon a neighbor to come pick them up. Traveling from the bus station to home in the neighbor's car, Frank once again repeated his saga, placing great emphasis on the providence and miracles of God in paving the way. At home, Bo related what all she had to sell to get the funds to go to New York. The cow. The chickens. Frank's tools by which he made a living to provide for his family. And some or her inherited jewelry. Both agreed it was necessary and would not be missed. They could buy another cow and chickens once Frank was back at work and they built up their nest egg again. They still had the acre of land and the house, even though there was still a mortgage on it.

Frank went to work as a carpenter's helper since he had no tools but knew the trade. Frank was earning enough to provide the necessities of life, butter, milk, eggs, sugar, flour, salt, electric bills, etc., Frank spent the rest of his earnings on tools. Mostly from a local pawn shop where he could get good used tools for a significantly lower price than new. Having worked with carpenter tools most of his life, Frank was a good judge of quality tools.

There was one thing that Frank did that brought joy to his heart. He found the jeweler in Rosenberg who had purchased Bo's prized necklace and earrings she had received as family heirlooms from her mother. The jeweler still had them for sale. Frank arranged with him (unbeknownst to Bo) to purchase them back on a time payment plan. Each week he would make a small payment on them and in time had them paid for. He secreted them away in a place unknown to Bo so that he could surprise her with them on their next anniversary.

He kept them secret from Bo until their anniversary, at which time he surprised her with an unexpected gift. When she opened the small, neatly wrapped present she let out a gasp and quickly broke into tears. She hugged and kissed Frank as more tears came down her cheeks. She had thought they were gone forever and did not think of them anymore. Other than getting Frank back from Ellis Island and their daughter Emilie, she said it was one of her best gifts.

Over time Frank acquired several hand saws, both cross cut and rip teeth sets. Two hammers, one a special roofing hammer, the other just a regular "claw" hammer. Several wood planes, including an almost new "jack" plane at half the original price, smoothing planes and finishing planes. And of course, he had to have a Brace and assorted bits for boring holes as needed. Along with a framing square and a level. He also bought a "plumb bob." To Frank a "plumb bob" was equivalent to a

Bible, it was a means of determining what was right and true. And a good tool box in which to store them. Frank could have made his own tool box but this one caught his eye and would allow him to put his skills to use earning money instead of building a tool box.

It was not very long before Frank was back out on his own, building and remodeling. There was always a demand for quality work and Frank's work was quality. He soon had a list of eager customers waiting on him. The fact that he had previously been an independent contractor and had a previous sterling reputation propelled his status and helped gain new customers.

Then hard times fell after WWII, the economy slowed down and there were many ex-servicemen returning home looking for work. Frank was able to hire some from time to time. He wanted to help those who helped protect the freedoms in America, which he appreciated even more since his experience in the Czech Republic. Everyone was trying to get ahead. Someone once said that climbing the ladder of success is not as difficult as getting through the crowd at the bottom of the ladder. Yet there were opportunities to be had for those willing to work hard.

Weeks turn into months and months into years. Over time Frank had been able to set aside some of his earnings to replenish what used to be in the kitchen cannister. Even more than what used to be there before Bo had to empty it to go to New York. He often thought of the events that led to his detainment in the Czech Republic and how God had worked to get him home.

Years passed by, but God had one more miracle in store for Frank. There was a long-abandoned house in Rosenberg that sat on the outside bank of a bend in the Brazos River. As the bank eroded more and more from the constant current of the river making that bend, the house became more and more in danger of sliding into the river. There the remains of the house would become a hazard. To prevent the house from falling into the river, the city had condemned it and put it up for bid.

Frank saw the ad in the paper and decided to take a look at it. Perhaps he could salvage enough lumber to build a garage or two and have materials left over for remodeling work. The house was old. Floors were made of tongue and groove heart pine, which was valued in the building trade. The framing was from rough cut lumber that measured true to the nominal size as opposed to the actual size after planning smooth. It was good lumber. One part of the roof leaked, causing severe water damage in two rooms. It was no prize and the condition scared some bidders off. Whatever the final bid was, it had to be paid in cash then and there, which left some of the bidders out as they did not have the funds. Frank did.

But Frank could see the potential and he bid on the house. As other bidders dropped out one by one, only Frank's bid remained and became the winning bid. He had bought a house, if you could call it a house. Now came the task of taking it apart in a way to save as much lumber as possible. After paying the winning bid, Frank did not have sufficient funds to pay a helper. He would have to do it himself with the aid of his new son who was now ten years old. It reminded him of how, he himself, had assisted his father Joseph when they first came to America.

Gathering his tools, ladders, and other equipment into his used 1949 pickup, he went to the house to begin tearing it down. He put a water sprinkler on the roof the day before to wet the house down. This caused the wood to swell and made pulling nails and prying boards apart easier. A trick he had learned from his father!

They set about removing the roofing and putting it to one side. It would have to be hauled to the dump and disposed of as one of the conditions of the sale was that the site had to be left clean. Then came the rafters. Frank put his son Henry in charge of cleaning the boards of nails and stacking them according to dimensions. It reminded Frank of his detail job in the military camp he escaped from so long ago.

On the inside of the house, Frank and his son began removing the doors by tapping the hinge pins out and slipping the door off the half of the hinge remaining on the frame. When they laid the third door down on the floor there suddenly came the distinctive clatter of coins hitting the floor. Some made humming a sound as they spun round and round on the hard wood floor! Some clashed against others. Some just rolled until they hit a wall and then fell flat.

Frank and Henry were astonished beyond belief! They were all five- and ten-dollar gold pieces! Examining the door to see where they came from, they discovered that whoever hid them had bored holes in the top of the door and then dropped the coins into the holes. What a perfect hiding place! The only way someone searching for something to steal from the occupants was to remove the door and tip it upside down! No thief would think of that or go to the trouble since they would have no reason to expect anything from the door other than a door. A door is a door, but not these doors. They hid something valuable and special.

They quickly gathered the coins up, placing them in the nail aprons they wore. They wanted to get the coins up before any "visitors," "curiosity seekers," or losing bidders came by to watch them tear the house down. Having discovered the secret hiding place, they went from door to door, running their fingers across the uppermost stile of the door feeling for similar holes. There was one other door that had such holes. They peered out the windows for evidence of any onlookers. Then, removing it from its hinges, they gently turned the door upside down and out poured more gold coins!

Frank was exhilarated as was Hank (Frank's nickname for his son Henry). Again, they gathered the coins into their nail aprons. They had secreted the previous finds away into the pickup and made sure the truck was locked. Now those coins had new companions as they did the same thing with the new finds. No other doors had any holes indicating the possibility of more to be found.

Frank said that they must continue working the entire day as if nothing out of the ordinary had occurred. Frank had borrowed a sixteen-foot trailer to help haul the cleaned lumber from the site. If it was not removed at the end of the day, scavengers may come by and haul it away for you, but not to where you desired! Having loaded all the lumber possible on the back of the truck and trailer, they excitedly traveled home to give Bo the good news.

Frank thought it best not to divulge the finding of the treasure trove to anyone. Bo questioned the ethics of the situation, after all they were not the ones who placed the coins there and were not the owners. In Frank's mind it was all okay. The house had been abandoned for years, who knows when the coins were put there or by whom, and where those people were. Obviously, the publication in the paper found no heirs and met the legal requirements for the city to sell the property at public auction.

Besides, Frank reasoned, he recalled an instance in the Bible where someone found buried treasure in a field. He then went and bought the field so that he could claim the treasure. He did not tell the seller that he found buried treasure in the field, and that is why he wanted to buy it. All of Frank's reasoning made sense to Bo. They agreed to not tell anyone.

To dispose of the coins, Frank drove to Houston to a numismatics shop that bought and sold coins. He only took five or six at a time. He also went to several different shops, sometimes selling as many as ten. Having disposed of all the coins, Frank used some of the money to pay off the mortgage on their home and one acre. He also bought another acre of land that was adjacent to theirs, paying cash for it. That gave him enough pasture to buy another cow. He bought another cow, so now he had the two cows he talked about with the old man.

As was his custom, he maintained a small garden behind the house. He expanded it somewhat. He used some of the lumber to increase the size of his garage, which was so small it would only accommodate his pickup. Now it was the size needed for two vehicles, but Frank used the extra space to store the remaining lumber out of the weather. Plus, a workbench and tool rack. The remainder of the house that Frank and his son Hank torn down had been stored in stacks held off the ground by sawhorses and covered with canvas. With the new storage provided by the garage addition, it could now be stored inside, out of the weather, to better preserve it. The remaining lumber almost filled the extra space he had built.

According to the contract in the purchase of the old house, they spent several days cleaning up the scraps and hauling them to the dump. It was back-breaking work and Frank realized he was not as young as he used to be! Stooping and bending, hoisting lumber up onto his shoulder was not as easy as it was in the past. It was a blessing to have Hank there to help him. It reminded him of when he used to work alongside of his

Papa. It was a pleasure to now have his son working alongside himself. It provided great opportunities to bond with his son, to teach him things and further his education about the world and about being a good citizen. But especially about being a good Christian.

Some years passed and Frank was in the shop working on a project. He attempted to lift a short but heavy beam up to his workbench when he felt a sharp pain in his chest. Setting it back down, he rested for a few minutes till the pain faded away. Then he tried it again and the sharp pain came back. After resting a second time, he went into the house and told Bo what had happened. She insisted that I go see a doctor.

The physician closest to their house was a family doctor, a generalist. Frank called to make an appointment, but when the assistant he talked with heard the reason why Frank wanted an appointment, she insisted that he come in right away.

So, Frank and Bo got in the truck and drove to the doctor's office. Hank was in school and would not be home until much later. After checking in and giving his medical history, which was almost non-existent, the doctor reviewed the information and gave Frank a quick exam, he paid particular attention to his heart by means of the stethoscope. Then he did it again, repeating the protocol of listening to Frank's chest and back while instructing him to take deep breaths and either hold it or breathe out. Also, while breathing normally.

The doctor's face was grim. It was not good news. The doctor would not state exactly what was wrong, only that he wanted Frank to go to a cardiac specialist at the local hospital. At the hospital, the specialist also gave Frank a similar exam and took some x-rays. The cardiac specialist wanted Frank admitted to the hospital for further testing, which included blood to be drawn and sent to the lab for analysis. Reluctantly Frank agreed and gave the truck keys to Bo so she could go home in time to be there when Hank got home from school.

Frank spent a restless night in the hospital. He missed his own bed. The food was not the same as what Bo cooked. The next day, a second doctor accompanied the cardiac specialist and had a consultation with Frank. The sum of the conversation amounted to the fact that Frank had several blocked vessels leading to and from his heart that were inoperable. Current day medicine had no remedy. He was told that he should go home, sit in his easy chair and lift nothing heavier than a newspaper! The news was devastating. Frank had so many things yet to do. He had always been so active. He did not want to be waited on as if he were an invalid.

Frank obeyed the doctors' orders. For two months he ate a bland diet, without salt. He sat in his chair. He read the newspaper, the Bible and watched TV. Bo could see that he was unhappy. He was not the same old Frank that she knew and loved. He seemed to be worse each day as part of the old Frank had to give way to the new. Then, after about two months, Frank folded up his newspaper, placed it neatly in the magazine rack by his chair, got his working shoes and put them on. Walking to the kitchen where Bo was washing dishes, he gave her a kiss and said, "I am going out and dig some potatoes." As he walked out the back door, he grabbed a burlap sack and his worn, weather-beaten straw hat. Putting on his hat, he paused at the back door and looked around. At last, he had a plotnic of his own and it had produced bountifully for him and his family. It was a beautiful, sunny day.

Bo kept washing dishes. She knew she would never be able to talk him out of what he was doing. She watched out the kitchen window with tears welling up in her eyes. She gave thanks to God for allowing Frank to be part of her life as tears began rolling down her cheeks. She watched helplessly as Frank got down on his knees and began grubbing up the ground where he had planted a row of potatoes. He dug up the earth for about ten feet, putting the potatoes he unearthed in the burlap sack. After about ten feet, Bo saw him stop. She stopped washing dishes and watched helplessly.

Frank grabbed a handfull of the rich Texas soil and squeezed it in his hand, and observed how the loam of the soil caused it to bind together into a clump, then lifting it up to his nose gave it a whiff. It was good soil! Frank loved the smell of the earth almost as much as the smell of fresh sawdust! Then, seeing a large potato he had halfway exposed during his grubbing he reached out with his other hand and freed it from the dirt. It was a good potato. It was large enough to fill his hand and had a beautiful symmetrical form to it. Frank thought about the potatoes he helped his father grow in the homeland that he did not get to see again. And the potatoes he helped the old man in Germany harvest. Bo watched out the kitchen window as Frank slumped forward, then fell on his right side….and slipped into eternity…to his one true homeland.

www.ingramcontent.com/pod-product-compliance
Lightning Source LLC
Chambersburg PA
CBHW040841010826
48978CB00012BB/857